This
Harry
book belongs to

· ·

SCELIDOSAURUS
(ske-LI-doh-SAW-rus)

TYRANNOSAURUS
(tie-RAN-oh-SAW-rus)

TRICERATOPS
(try-SER-a-tops)

STEGOSAURUS
(STEG-oh-SAW-rus)

PTERODACTYL
(TER-oh-DAC-til)

APATOSAURUS
(a-PAT-oh-SAW-rus)

ANCHISAURUS
(AN-ki-SAW-rus)

In memory of Mason Jones and for all of his friends
at Deri Primary School, Bargoed, who miss him very much - I.W.

For Calum - A.R.

PUFFIN BOOKS
Published by the Penguin Group: London, New York, Ireland, Australia, Canada, India, New Zealand and South Africa
Penguin Books Ltd, Registered Offices: 80 Strand, London WC2R 0RL, England

www.penguin.com

Published in Puffin Books 2006
Published in this edition 2006
3 5 7 9 10 8 6 4 2
Text copyright © Ian Whybrow, 2006
Illustrations copyright © Adrian Reynolds, 2006
Manufactured in China
ISBN-13: 978-0-141-50005-8
ISBN-10: 0-141-50005-0

Harry and the Dinosaurs Go To School

Ian Whybrow and Adrian Reynolds

PUFFIN

It was a big day for Harry. He was starting at his new school.
He was very excited because one of his friends, Charlie,
was starting that day too.

Stegosaurus said he didn't want to go. Not after
Triceratops told him about no Raaahs in class.
Mum said not to worry, school would be fine.

Harry blew his whistle just like a teacher.
  He said, "In twos, holding hands, my dinosaurs.
No talking and jump in the bucket."

The dinosaurs did what Harry said.
  All except Stegosaurus. He was so
nervous, all his plates were rattling.
  Harry had to give him a special stroke.

Sam said, "You can't take dinosaurs to school, stupid!"
That's why her toast fell on the floor.

Mum took Harry to school.

Mrs Rance was waiting at the classroom door when
Harry and Mum got there.
"Hello, Harry," she said. "Welcome to your new school."
They all said goodbye to the mums and dads.

Then Mrs Rance showed Harry the coat pegs.
"You can leave your lunchbox here too," she said.
Harry was too shy to say could he have his bucket back.
That's why his dinosaurs got left outside the classroom.

Harry missed his dinosaurs, so he didn't like the classroom.
He didn't like the home corner, or his special work tray.

And he felt sorry for another new boy with a digger
who cried when his mum went home.
The boy wouldn't say one single word, not even his name.

Harry sort of liked the playground at playtime.
But it wasn't much fun, even the monkey bars –
not without his dinosaurs.

Back in class, the digger boy still wouldn't speak.
   "Maybe he wants to go to the toilet," Harry suggested.
"I'll show him where it is, shall I?"
   Mrs Rance said good idea, how thoughtful.

All the way to the toilet the boy kept quiet.
 It was the same on the way back, till they got to the coats.
Then they heard a voice, very sad and very soft.
 "Raaaaaaaaaaah!" it said.

"That's my dinosaurs," said Harry. "They miss me. Would you like to see them?"

The boy nodded so Harry said, "This is my Apatosaurus and my Anchisaurus and my Scelidosaurus.

This is Triceratops and Tyrannosaurus. Pterodactyl is the baby. Wait! Where's Stegosaurus?"

"Jump out, Stegosaurus," called Harry. "Don't be shy!"

But Stegosaurus wanted a whisper.

"Ah," said Harry. "Stegosaurus says he will come out but only if he can have a ride on your digger."

And do you know what? The boy nodded and passed it over.

When Harry and the boy got back, Mrs Rance said,
"Oh good! Dinosaurs. I love dinosaurs. Do they Raaah?"

"RAAAAAAAAAAAAAH!" said the dinosaurs
and blew all the windows open.
   "My goodness!" said Mrs Rance. "That *was* a Raaah!"

They all sat down in the classroom.
  "Now, we're going to make new labels for our
coat pegs," said Mrs Rance. "Hands up who knows
how to write their name?"

The boy with the digger put up his hand.
 "And what are you going to write?" smiled Mrs Rance.
 "Jackosaurus!" said the boy.
 It was the very first word he had spoken all day.
And what a good joke, too!
 All the other children laughed and laughed.

Harry felt very happy.
  Charlie, Harry and their new friend Jack sat down
together at a table with the dinosaurs.

They laughed and they Raaahed
and they made beautiful labels
to show where they belonged.

ENDOSAURUS

SCELIDOSAURUS

(ske-LI-doh-SAW-rus)

TYRANNOSAURUS

(tie-RAN-oh-SAW-rus)

TRICERATOPS

(try-SER-a-tops)

STEGOSAURUS

(STEG-oh-SAW-rus)

PTERODACTYL

(TER-oh-DAC-til)

APATOSAURUS

(a-PAT-oh-SAW-rus)

ANCHISAURUS

(AN-ki-SAW-rus)

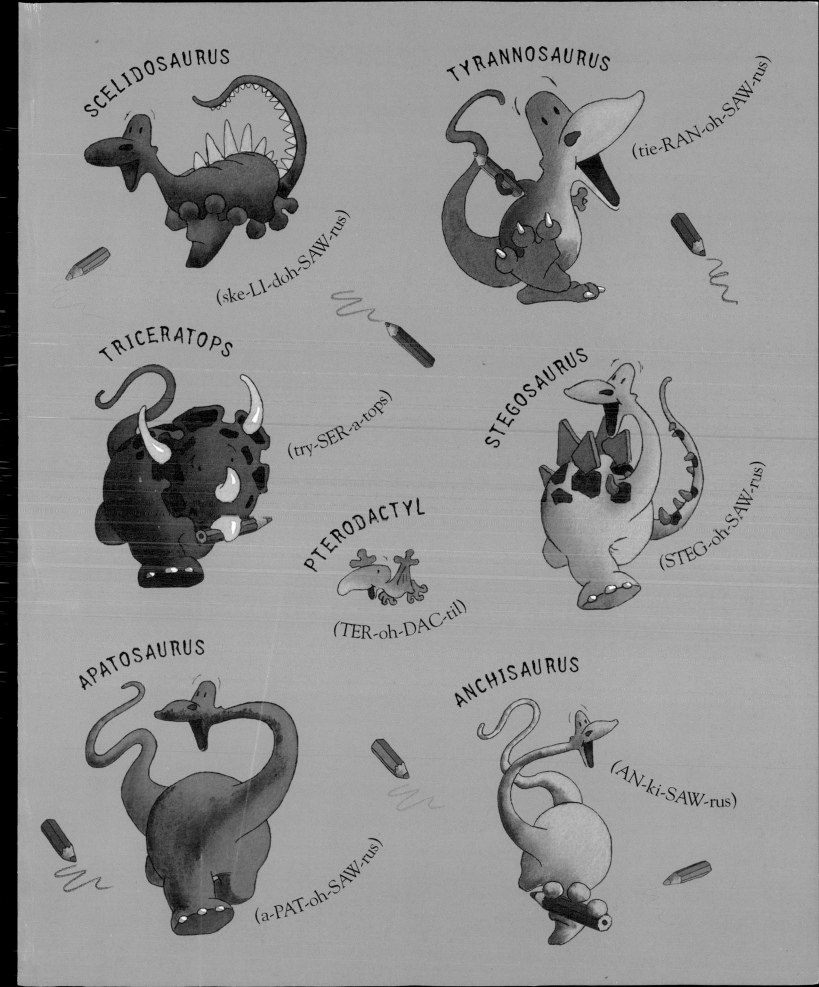

SCELIDOSAURUS

(ske-LI-doh-SAW-rus)

TYRANNOSAURUS

(tie-RAN-oh-SAW-rus)

TRICERATOPS

(try-SER-a-tops)

STEGOSAURUS

(STEG-oh-SAW-rus)

PTERODACTYL

(TER-oh-DAC-til)

APATOSAURUS

(a-PAT-oh-SAW-rus)

ANCHISAURUS

(AN-ki-SAW-rus)

Look out for all of Harry's adventures!

Harry and the Bucketful of Dinosaurs
Harry finds some old, plastic dinosaurs and cleans them, finds out their names and takes them everywhere with him – until, one day, they get lost... Will he ever find them?

ISBN 0140569804

Harry and the Snow King
There's just enough snow for Harry to build a very small snow king. But then the snow king disappears – who's kidnapped him?

ISBN 0140569863

Harry and the Robots
Harry's robot is sent to the toy hospital to be fixed, so Harry and Nan decide to make a new one. When Nan has to go to hospital, Harry knows just how to help her get better!

ISBN 0140569820

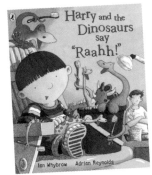

Harry and the Dinosaurs say "Raahh!"
Harry's dinosaurs are acting strangely. They're hiding all over the house, refusing to come out... Could it be because today is the day of Harry's dentist appointment?

ISBN 0140569812

Harry and the Dinosaurs Romp in the Swamp
Harry has to play at Charlie's house and doesn't want to share his dinosaurs. But when Charlie builds a fantastic swamp, Harry and the dinosaurs can't help but join in the fun!

ISBN 0140569847

Harry and the Dinosaurs make a Christmas Wish
Harry and the dinosaurs would *love* to own a duckling. They wait till Christmas and make a special wish, but Santa leaves them something even more exciting...!

ISBN 0141380179 (hbk)
ISBN 0140569529 (pbk)

ISBN 0140569839

ISBN 0140569855

Harry and the Dinosaurs play Hide-and-Seek
Harry and the Dinosaurs have a Very Busy Day
Join in with Harry and his dinosaurs for some peep-through fold-out fun! These exciting books about shapes and colours make learning easy!